My Dog Wants to Be a Cat

By

Linda Laudone

Illustrated by

Jacob Scheyder

Andres & Blanton

My Dog Wants to Be a Cat
Published by Andres & Blanton
Niantic, Connecticut

ISBN 978-0-9966721-0-8

Printed in the United States of America

www.andresblanton.com

10 9 8 7 6 5 4 3 2 1

To my loves:
Ayden, Donovan, Ella and Alex

My dog wants to be a cat.
Belle is not too pleased with that.

Fancy, free, and on her own,
Belle just wants to be alone.

Abby likes to play all day,
Always getting in the way.

Belle sits on the window sill.

Guess who joins her? Abby will!

Scratching with her tiny toes,

Abby tries to touch Belle's nose.

Resting in the rocking chair,

Abby jumps up - what a pair!

Belle takes time to grab a treat.

Abby thinks it's time to eat.

Belle decides to hide, instead.

Abby finds her - bumps her head!

Belle just wants to take a nap.

Abby crawls into her lap.

Belle is careful not to splash.

Abby dives in with a crash!

Belle goes to her happy place.
Sometimes friends
Just need their space.

One thing separates the two.
Can you guess what dogs can't do?

About the Author

Linda Laudone was born and raised in southeastern Connecticut. She works as a paraprofessional with special needs students.

The adorable friendship between my dog, Abby, and my cat, Belle, inspired me to share their story. Despite their obvious differences, they loved each other unconditionally.

Special thanks to Susie and Jacob Scheyder for helping me accomplish my dream!

Jacob Scheyder, the illustrator, has a degree in film production. His artwork can be found in movies, on T-shirts and in educational materials.

A portion of the proceeds from this book will benefit animal shelters in southeastern Connecticut.

CPSIA information can be obtained at www.ICGtesting.com
Printed in the USA
LVOW05s2142230815

451263LV00032B/832/P